The Shifty Champion

The Shifty Magician

Cathy Smith

Published by Cathy Smith, 2020.

THE SHIFTY CHAMPION

First edition. June 16, 2020.

Copyright © 2020 Cathy Smith.

ISBN: 979-8230244905

Written by Cathy Smith.

Table of Contents

Chapter 1-Help Wanted 1

Chapter 2-The Job Vacancy 6

Chapter 3-The Debut 12

Chapter 4-The Shattered Mirror 17

Chapter 5-The Menial Minion 23

Chapter 6-A Cease and Desist Letter 29

Chapter 7-The Letter is Returned 35

Chapter 8-The Black Knight 40

Chapter 9-Delivering A Warning.. 46

Chapter 10-The Premier Apprentice in the Trade............. 52

Chapter 11-Now That You've Proven Yourself................... 57

About the Author... 63

Chapter 1-Help Wanted

My master promoted me from minion to apprentice. So far this meant added responsibilities and better pay and commissions.

Damien still made me do the household chores and errands, though he'd added classes to my workload. Plus, my pose as his man of business was too lucrative for him to delegate to someone else.

My current skills were modest. I could jinx, had intuition and brewed the simple medical and housecleaning potions. These potions were good to keep in stock but below a master magician's dignity. So Damien taught me how to brew them than left it to me to keep them in stock.

I could use most magical tools, which the Trade considered a job skill too. So far I was most proficient at using a cleaning wand I found at Quinn's Emporium, which catered to the Trade. It was more useful to me than the wands that made grandiose claims of power. Damien disapproved of wands but allowed me to use this one.

He'd complained that the magical broom was "typical" when I bought it, but I assured him it was for cleaning. Making the broom sweep for me unnerved my cat familiar Scrappy. Of course, I'd been forced to shoo him away twice with said broom, and he held a grudge against it.

He growled at it as if it was an unwary mouse. I ignored him as I commanded it to sweep up his used sand into a dustpan and place it into an empty bag. Then use the wand to pour a fresh bin in his sandbox.

Damien's raven Tobias considered my housework a spectacle worthy of heckling. He snorted when I moved onto the dirty dishes.

I picked up a dish that now had a mirror-like shine. "Do you want me to build character and do household the old-fashioned way?" I asked him.

He sighed at this. Only light magicians cared about "character."

"I have only two hands, Tobias and Damien's given me a sales quota to meet. How am I to find prospects and keep this townhouse clean if I have to do everything myself?" I asked him.

He fluttered his wings. "These cleaning tools are lightside tricks. They'll refuse to clean up dark magic residue."

I shrugged. "Maybe so but there's no harm in giving them simple household tasks to lighten my workload."

Indeed, I'd go through every room once a week to magic away the dusting. It got the job done fast but was as exhausting as doing things by hand. Thanks to these factors only two to three rooms got cleaned in a day.

Some rooms were big and messy. I wasn't able to work on any other rooms when I cleaned them.

"We need a new minion. It can't be good for your career as a black magician's apprentice to be so reliant on a lightside trick."

I shuddered at this. I'd been a minion, and I'd hate to inflict that duty on someone else.

"Do you think I could find a minion that operates the magical cleaning tools?" I asked Tobias.

"They'd think you were teasing them by only letting them use cleaning tools." Tobias said.

"Not everyone in the Trade wants to be some grand master." I was an apprentice, and I had no such ambition myself. There were still worthwhile magical skills worth cultivating though. They were still useful even if they didn't give me ultimate power. "Surely someone would be glad to use a modest tool for cleaning?"

Tobias laughed. "You make it sound so innocent and sensible."

"And you sound like some churchgoer who thinks we use all magic for evil purposes." I countered.

He snorted at this.

I took the bag of used sand into the trash before I fed the familiars for the day. Tobias didn't want my hands getting dirty before I served his food so had no snide comments on the wand.

I laid out Scrappy's fish and last night's meat leftover's for Tobias. Tobias preferred carrion but made do with aged meat. The animals stopped watching me once their needs were met.

Then it was time to wash my hands and make a light breakfast for Damien. Brew some coffee, fry some ham, slice a grapefruit and toast some bread. Damien ate breakfast at home. Luckily for me, they served luncheon and supper at the social events and venues he attended.

I collected the periodicals from the front step and the mail. Then sorted out the mail. It took fine motor control and discretion to cook meals, sort the mail, so it wasn't worth using the wand on that.

My promotion meant I received various trade related flyers and notices. My master received those and letters from women. It was like he was perpetually receiving valentines. Some of them were elegant. Others were garish.

I set the women's letters aside. It was hard for me to tell who was in favor and who wasn't, so I didn't cull them. That's why I made sure there was an empty garbage bin at the breakfast table, so Damien could sort them himself. However, I noticed there was one feminine hand that wrote on silver paper. They sealed their letters with a diamond signet. He always accepted these letters, no matter who his current favorite was. I assumed she must either be beautiful or so powerful that Damien dared not cross her.

I laid everything out for Damien and poured out a coffee for myself. When Tobias finished his breakfast he flew onto his perch in the breakfast room to await the day's orders.

Scrappy found a sunny spot in the room and took his morning nap. He was my familiar and should've awaited my orders. I was lucky he stuck close by me at all.

I gathered my courage while I waited for Damien Rathschild to make his appearance. Housework was my duty as a minion, but shouldn't be now that I was an apprentice.

It took more than one person to maintain a home of this size. The most misanthropic black magician I'd ever known had had household servants. Surely Damien Rathschild could find discreet and loyal household staff? Making me do the household chores was a false economy.

Such were my furious thoughts as I prepared my argument. It'd do no good to complain about my duties. He couldn't care less about fairness. He believed in making the best use of his resources, though. My hours of work as his man of business was too valuable to waste with hours of drudgery. Every hour I spent cleaning this townhouse was one less hour I billed to our clients.

Damien came down and sorted his correspondence first. I had to wait for him to sort the letters before he talked to me. He deposited half the letters in the trash bin. Then he set the other half aside and opened them one by one. I started when he shoved the open letters to me. "I want you to pay these invoices."

"Invoices?" He was so striking I assumed his appeal to women was natural charisma. Though I knew he was always generous to his current favorite.

Seeing my frown, he sighed, "The demimonde are my best informants on my enemies' activities. I disguise my payments as compensation for services rendered. Anyone who knows of my payments assumes I'm one of their many admirers."

He tapped one letter in particular. It was one with a silver diamond sigil. "Mathilde Kildare has a commission for us. A mystery man has become the patron of too many younger enchantresses. She wants us to investigate him."

"Is he collecting a harem?" I asked.

Damien sighed. "Mathilde doesn't care if he's gathering them for himself. However, he may be grooming young ladies to sell to other buyers."

"She thinks he's a white slaver?" I asked.

"It's happened to enchantresses before." He shrugged.

I knew better to refuse him, but used this as an opening. "My current workload means I may not give this task as much attention as it deserves."

His brows rose. "You have other commissions?"

I set my cup of coffee down and ticked off my duties on my hand.

"No, but my housekeeping duties take up a quarter of my time and energy. I spend another quarter on my man of business duties. Then there are my classes. This limits my time for investigations."

I figure the housekeeping duties are the one negotiable variable."

Tobias opened his beak in prelude to chanting, "You will soon be carrion."

Scrappy opened his eyes and his ears perked forward.

Damien sniffed as if he already smelled a stench." I refuse to live in a garbage heap."

"I'm not suggesting you lower your personal hygiene standards."

His brows rose as he sipped his coffee. "Then what are you suggesting?"

"Josiah Nesfer was the most misanthropic black magician in Ilan. If he could have a household full of servants, I don't see why we can't hire a housekeeper for this establishment. Every hour I have to spend on housecleaning is one less hour I can bill our clients." I said.

"You are free to hire any freelancers you want to outsource tasks to. However, I expect you to handle their compensation, and manage their job performance." Damien said.

"Is that a yes or no?"

"Those are the conditions I insist on if you hire a housekeeper." He said as I sighed in relief. "You can use your extra billable hours to earn money for their salary."

I nodded at this. I expected nothing less than this and was confident I could adhere to these terms.

Chapter 2-The Job Vacancy

Call me selfish, but finding a housekeeper took precedence for me. I'd investigate the potential white slaver when I settled the issue.

I rated black magicians the same as criminals and there were well off criminals I knew who had servants too.

My former employer's servants knew what he was and served him well. Surely he'd know where to find loyal employees in the Underworld.

"I've been promoted at work and need someone to take over my housekeeping duties. How can I find someone reliable?"

"Most people view servants as human furniture," Benny James shrugged when I asked him for advice.

"But you're not a regular employer. What's stopping them from informing on you?"

He sighed. "I have three rules for servants. A fair number don't care what you do as long as you're discreet. Keeping up your own appearance helps them keep up theirs."

"Second: Don't be cheap. Don't expect them to work for prestige. There's always a chance your enemies will outbid you. Yet, you don't want them so impoverished they have to supplement their income. You don't want them informing on you to get a living wage.

I thought of Damien and his dark magic rituals and duels. "What about others who are more hardcore than you? What do they do?"

"You can always take in someone from off the streets. Someone who's street smart but looking for better. They'll be willing to do what it takes to stay off the streets if they're young. If they're older, they may see domestic service to a successful criminal as a retirement plan. Housework would be getting off lightly..."

When I presented Benny's suggestions to Damien he said, "I don't want street riffraff in my house. Find someone respectable whose sympathetic to the Trade."

Which is why I went to Chauncey. He was a bottom-feeder and "sympathetic to the Trade." Perhaps I could even get him to accept a position in the household?

Chauncey snorted at this. "I'm not as hard up as that. You can put an ad in a Trade periodical. There's people who love being around magic even if they can't work magic themselves."

I sighed. "Do you think it'd be cruel to give them a cleaning wand and broom to work with?"

His brows rose.

"I've been using them myself."

He snickered. "You could tell them you're offering basic magic instruction. It might get you more applicants."

Calling the use of magical cleaning tools "basic instruction" was an exaggeration. However, I'd been a conman before I met Damien and included it in my job ad, anyway.

Most periodicals refused my ads except for Warlock's Weekly. Warlock's Weekly was the Trade's guiltiest pleasure. Its Top 10 lists were beloved by magic practitioners. Even if most of them decried the newspaper as a yellow rag.

Younger members of the Trade supported it. They said, "Warlock's Weekly dares to print what's only whispered about."

They alerted me to the Trade's opinion of me and my master when I checked for my job ad the following week. They rated Damien and me number one in our respective divisions.

This could've been high praise until I read the accompanying editorial:

Let's admit that Rathschild and his apprentice did a public service. Josiah Nesfer was a public menace. That's why I've assigned the top spot in their divisions.

My blood pressure rose to see my ad at the bottom of the page with my offer of basic instruction in magic in italics.

"They're accusing you of murdering Josiah Nesfer and of me being your accomplice." I sputtered as I threw the newspaper on the breakfast table.

Damien's brows rose. "You're my apprentice. Of course, you're my accomplice. I'm more troubled by your offer to teach basic magic instruction to the applicants."

I shrugged. "I'd show them how to use the cleaning wand and magic broom. I may also get them to brew our homemade cleaning materials."

Damien scowled. "You'll teach them how to use a magic broom to fly? "

"I'm talking about the broom I use to sweep the floor for me." I said. "This is a big townhouse for one person to clean. I assume the applicant will have lesser skills than me. Keeping it clean would take up all their work hours. Besides that, you know magic has its costs. The tools don't demand blood, but it takes magical power and physical energy to use them. Let's find some loyal drudge to do it for us. I won't increase my skills in jinxing if I keep diverting my talents into simple housecleaning."

He grunted at this. "I want you to get strong enough to hex people. It's unseemly for a black magician's apprentice to be proficient in cleaning spells."

I nodded. "That's what I mean. I hate to think of what sort of applicants we'll get for the job ad after this editorial. If we get any applicants at all."

He patted my shoulder. "I find helping the enchantresses always generates good will. I may even ask Mathilde to recommend someone to us."

DAMIEN MEANT HIS COMMENT about the enchantresses as a hint to start their commission. However, there was one resume submitted for the housekeeping position the next day. I wanted to interview them before I got to work researching that greedy protector.

The application had a brochure for Menials & Minions sent to our address with a resume attached to it. It tempted me to throw it out on principle, but I decided not to.

I looked over Tara Halliday's application. I heard the author's voice every time I read a piece of their writing. Her voice lilted and chirped like a bird's. Which told me she was young. Hopefully she was able-bodied too. Though I hoped her brain wasn't as light as her voice. Damien wouldn't like it if she were bird-brained.

I kept rereading her resume to see if I could read more into it. The voice wasn't giving me enough to work with. I hunted up the scrying mirror and Tobias got suspicious when I asked where it was.

"I have one applicant and want to see what they look like before I invite them in for a job interview."

"Huh?"

"The scrying mirror works with my author's voice trick to show me the author's face, remember?" I sighed.

His wings fluttered at this. "You're using the author's trick as a screening tool?"

"Yes," I couldn't see why this should embarrass me.

"Then I suggest we use it to simplify the background check for that protector. He must've sent a note or two with his gifts to Mathilde Kildare's Diamonds of the First Water."

I nodded at this. "That's right. It'd be best to keep things simple."

My promise to look over the protector's notes won me the scrying mirror and ear horn. "I'll tell the Master it's best that you keep it in your office if it's a screening tool." Which is how I got to put them into an unused office, which was a spare room I had to clean before I could use it.

I reread the brochure. Its promises sounded more impressive. It paired the bass voice with the image of a white-haired patriarch with bushy hair and whiskers. He wore a spotless white suit that was impossible to attain in Beldon's smog without magical aid. He looked too grand for this sideline.

Tara Halliday was a pert little chick. Who looked too frail for the job I had in mind for her. She promised "satisfaction" with her services with a bob that made her bosom jiggle and a sly wink.

I snorted. There were some gentlemen who demanded "extra" from their female servants. It looked like that this "extra" was all Tara would offer me.

It was just my luck Damien came in just then and saw her jiggles.

He snorted, "What are you reading?"

I held up the job application. Damien skimmed through and sighed. "Don't hire this wench. You'd offend her if you expected her to do any housework."

I motioned to Scrappy, who slept at my feet. "I already have a pet."

"Scrappy's a familiar and should do more than capture mice in this household." Damien said. Scrappy howled at this while Tobias snickered.

"And he will once I find a housekeeper and can concentrate on my studies. I don't have time to train him when I'm so busy doing housework." I said.

Scrappy meowed agreement. Tobias snorted, "You sluggard."

Damien shook his head. "I will have Mathilde recommend someone suitable to us. People in and out of the Trade are eager to win their favors. Her endorsement help us attract qualified applicants."

"We'll still get paid, right? It's not good to always barter in Trade."

He gestured to the scrying mirror. "I demanded monetary payment if this task required extensive research. Tobias reminded me of how the mirror supplement's your author's voice trick. I'll propose a simple trade for a trade. We'll get a note from that collector. I'll draw a sketch, so they can identify him."

My master was an accomplished sketch artist. Though he preferred to use it to keep accurate records rather than create art. It wasn't something he wanted too well known.

He had high hopes for photography, which was another one of his hobbies. However, it wasn't up to his standards for speed and accuracy yet. Especially compared to his colored pencil sketches.

We sent a request for notes from the collector. Mathilde sent us a sample and Damien did a colored pencil sketch of him that night. He used the image that appeared in the scrying mirror as I read the note out.

"That's weird."

Damien's brows rose. "Isn't my technique up to your standards?" Tobias smacked his beak and Scrappy's fur stood on end.

"No, that face looks like the one from the Menial's & Minion's brochure. This one had that resume attached to it."

I lifted the brochure into the mirror and that man read off the benefits of his company's services. Damien compared the face in the mirror to the one he'd just created.

Then I held out that saucy miss's resume. "Does this count as white slavery?" I asked.

Damien sniffed in distaste. "Men often over-promise services to enchantresses. It's disappointing, but not a felony. The enchantresses won't like the fact he funnels his proteges to a domestic agency."

He drew a quick sketch of the man from the brochure and letter and made me hand copy the documents' contents. We enclosed that in our reply.

A letter came from Mathilde two days later. *It sounds like your apprentice is a talented young man. I'd like him to show his abilities at a cotillion I'm hosting. Make sure you bring the documents and the scrying mirror to the exhibition. My*

Diamonds won't believe your report without them. They must see Shelton Sharpe demonstrate his abilities.

She enclosed an invitation for my debut.

Tobias whistled. "You'll establish your reputation in the Trade if you can deliver the goods."

Damien nodded at this. "You must buy a new evening suit for the event."

Chapter 3-The Debut

I bought a new suit from the best tailor in Beldon for the occasion. Damien ordered me to hand polish the scrying mirror and its ear horn. Then I hand-delivered it to the Diamond Palace on the night of my debut.

The fact I had to perform for the guests confused me. "Am I the honored guest or the entertainment?"

"I want you to conduct yourself as a prestige performer contracted for a premier class event. You're performing but need to mingle with the guests once the event is over."

"Make sure you bring your tobacco. I want you to keep your wits about you."

Damien's mentor was a New World wizard. Tobacco was a medicine plant among his people. Damien learned, and taught me, to carry a pinch in my pocket to counter negative magical energies.

My author's trick seemed too pedestrian to be worth all this fuss. It wasn't as if I was a brilliant orator, even if that letter writer was a great showman. Though debunking a protector's claims required flair for my report to be believed.

The debut was to be over a weekend and included accommodation in the Palace. The Diamond Palace was a mansion in the theater district. A very well appointed townhouse, even if no Quality Lady would dare to set up a household in the district.

The house servants took my luggage and the scrying mirror from our hansom cab. The butler lead us to the foyer. There was a roomful of ladies waiting for us. They were lead by an elegant grande dame who you could tell had been a beauty in her time. Her eyes were a bright piercing blue, and she carried herself like a queen expecting homage. She still cut a respectable figure in her black satin gown but kept her bosom covered with a high collar.

The ladies descended to the front from a staircase as Mathilde called their names out. "These are my Diamonds of the First Water."

"Crystal." was a platinum blonde miss who wore a crystal covered gown. She was beautiful, but I thought her choice of clothing was overkill for the occasion.

"Rose." was a bold redhead who gave me a knowing wink when I stared at her too long. I had to avert my eyes from her cleavage, which was downright captivating.

"Then there's Goldie." Who wore a gold lame dress that matched her hair. Her smile was dazzling.

I'd never seen such glamour in my life, but it did what it was supposed to do. The tobacco gave off a scent as it fought off their allure. These women were grand and didn't appear cheap and overblown to me. Then again, I'd only attended the cheap seats before.

"These three are being tutored by me at the moment before they create their own salons," Mathilde said.

"It's a pleasure to meet you all," I said.

"We all wanted to meet the man capable of reuniting the Diamonds of the First Water for the first time in a year." Rose sighed.

Crystal laughed, and her voice was as clear as a bell. "Be prepared with a deluge of notes from secret admirers they'll want deciphered."

"Some want you to to solve an intriguing mystery. Others want to sic their protectors on their letter senders." Goldie giggled.

Damien frowned at this.

I wanted to tell them I'd want to be put on retainer if I did this much work. Instead, I smiled at them. "I'm afraid my current duties may keep me too busy to give you the attention you deserve."

I would've said a plain "no" to anyone else. However, I was in the habit of not refusing a Lady of Quality. Whether because I wanted their favor or else they had influential menfolk. Diamonds of the First Water were bound to have a lot of pull in Ilan society. I thought it best to operate under the same policy I used for Ladies of Quality.

"Yes," Damien agreed. "He's just been promoted and needs time to learn his new duties."

"We'd hire you on as a contractor, of course," Mathilde spoke up.

Goldie nodded, "We know a true professional can't live off of traded favors."

Crystal chimed in, "Though we want you to show us your abilities first."

I HAD TO CHANGE INTO a dress suit for the evening. Which was a jacket with a longer tail and a cravat that was too frothy for my taste. I combed my hair smooth but refused to put pomade on my locks.

Damien did the same and cut a more impressive figure than me. We were given seats of honor in front of a podium with red velvet drapes behind us. They set the scrying mirror and ear horn up next to me.

Damien frowned to see a sketchpad, pencil and eraser were set at an easel in front of his seat.

As soon as we took a seat, a line formed of ladies and their escorts. Ushers had set up a barrier to control the traffic. It barred entry at our table at the moment but would become a flood once they lowered the barriers.

The man who overlooked the security detail was tall and imposing. He gave me a look, and his eyes narrowed. My ginger hair was a sign of untrustworthiness among some people. It was a tell-tale sign among those that follow physiognomy. Even if its bright color drew people with the instinct of magpies to me.

The man walked up to us to speak. Damien frowned for a second, but then he guarded his face.

"Fletcher," Damien said. "Are you here on business or pleasure?"

Fletcher grimaced. "I agreed to be the head of security for this event if I got to sample your apprentice's skills first."

He threw a note on the table before me. I looked to Damien, and he nodded. As soon as I touched the paper a snide snively voice said, "I'd like to hire you to dance for me, you naughty girl. This five dollar note is my down payment on a private performance."

Fletcher glared into the mirror as it was being said. Damien wrinkled his nose in distaste.

Mathilde frowned.

Some ladies either rolled their eyes or nodded "no." Others shuddered, and their escorts held their shoulders.

Fletcher slapped down a note and said. "I want you to draw me a picture of the letter writer."

Seeing Damien frown at this command, Mathilde said. "I've got a sketch artist on staff who can make a sketch within five minutes. Can you come forward, Billy?"

A thin, sensitive looking youth with trembling hands came forward. He set up an easel and pallet. I had to keep rereading the note, so he could capture the man's face.

Fletcher took the picture and said. "We'll be consulting with you on other cases."

"Cases?" I asked. "

I gestured at the mirror. "I have the author's voice talent but will it count as evidence in an Ilan Court of Law?"

Fletcher smiled at me. "It will in the Watcher's Circle in Petrack. Your Master will have to take you in to register you within the next six weeks."

He tipped his hat to me as Damien scowled but didn't protest against this pronouncement.

The ladies had similar letters to show me. Some squealed in delight at the sight of their secret admirers. Or else groaned in disgust when their hopes were dashed.

Ladies' escorts often muttered, "I know who to challenge to a duel now."

A new line developed as some women and young men lined up to talk to Mathilde. They glanced at me and muttered to her. She'd give a nod and then called out, "Freida."

Her personal secretary came up to her with a legal pad and mechanical pen to write names. Freida was pretty but looked like a strict schoolmarm. She had thin lips, spectacles and a tight bun with every hair in place.

I barely had time to notice this, but it meant that the demonstration took less time than I thought it would.

The secretary laid the list she'd made on the table in front of me. "We'll set up a suite for private consultations at this room number." She pointed to a room number.

Damien's brows rose.

Freida smiled at him. "They're willing to pay three times the going rate for discretion. I was thinking we could prevail upon you to make the sketches yourself?"

Damien nodded at this.

I shuddered. It'd been a busy evening already, but at least Mathilde laid a generous table for us after my work.

Just when I was about to relax a black haired man with a Van Dyke walked up to our table. He had sharp black eyes that were as piercing as Damien's. "I don't know if I should congratulate you on a talented new apprentice or for a first class scrying mirror." His smile was snide.

Damien gestured at the scrying mirror. "You're welcome to try it yourself, Samwell."

"Perhaps, I shall." He said.

He held a letter out in front of the mirror. All he got back was his own reflection.

Samwell scowled. "How do I know it isn't attuned to you and your apprentice?"

Damien took the letter in his hand and held it up. The mirror showed only his reflection. He motioned to me. "Do you want my apprentice to show you the author?"

Samwell took the letter back and stomped out of the room. Damien's grin told me my modest talent was bringing me more notice than I wanted.

Chapter 4-The Shattered Mirror

Everyone retired to their suite for the evening. "My Diamonds prefer to entertain their escorts in private. Your debut was the early evening entertainment."

She'd invited us to a private dinner in her suite, but it was a business event. Crystal was present. I didn't think she'd ever lack an escort if she wanted one, and I hadn't expected her presence at the dinner.

She hadn't given a packet of letters to Freida. "I don't want to accept a new protector until they've been vetted."

Freida took the letters and included them in an overflowing box of notes they wanted me to review.

She then handed me an appointment book for my weekend's appointments. I groaned to see it was completely filled out. However, the sight of the fees assigned to each reading was very gratifying. I'd earn more in one weekend than I normally raised in one week.

Damien took the book from me and flipped through it. "I knew your talent was useful but didn't think it'd be in such high demand."

"Fletcher wants to put you on retainer, and there will be a meeting to work out terms."

I frowned. "I'm being hired as a consultant by a police force? Isn't that expecting too much of my mediocre talent?"

Mathilde smiled at me. "The Angel Investor is fond of taunting his rivals with anonymous notes.

The Watchers investigate death threats and taunts from suspects in their investigations. Your talent means they can't remain anonymous. Though Fletcher's superiors will want your accuracy rated first. It won't be considered proper evidence in their tribunals otherwise."

I shuddered at this.

Damien bit his lip. "I came here as a personal favor to you, Mathilde. I didn't expect my apprentice to be co-opted like this."

"He'll only be your apprentice for seven years, Damien. He needs to establish a reputation separate from you."

Damien grimaced, "He's an apprentice. He shouldn't be expected to do a master's work so early in his career."

Mathilde's brows rose. "Yet, you use him to track down anyone who sends you death threats."

Death threats for my master used to arrive with great frequency, but had fallen down ever since I developed my author's voice trick.

Damien sighed. "Which I regret not keeping to myself. I offered you a personal favor I didn't expect a Watcher to be present at this debut."

Mathilde shrugged. "Fletcher didn't like the fact I was calling in a third party to the investigation. Shelton would need to be classified and rated, eventually. I expected this occasion to be more congenial than the mandatory exam."

"Well, you were wrong." Damien said. Dinner was served, and that ended the conversation. There was an awkward silence as we ate.

IT WAS A RELIEF WHEN we retired early. My performance and the tense dinner tired me. My intuition made me oversensitive to everyone's moods.

However, Damien, Crystal and I inspected my suite for the upcoming interviews first.

My foot gave off a crunch when I stepped into the room. I looked down to see shards of broken glass in the velvet carpet. "Hm." The scrying mirror was shattered.

"No," Crystal cried out in horror. "How can you hear the author's voice if your tools are broke?"

"I can always hear an author's voice. The mirror helped me to see their face. The ear horn was more for everyone else's convenience than mine."

Crystal gasped in relief at this and rubbed the goosebumps on her forearm's flesh. She closed her eyes. "Can you get results from any scrying tool? Are you only attuned to the mirror?"

"I learned its quirks, but I should be able to make any scrying mirror work for me. I bought the mirror at Errol's pawn shop, and he had me try out various mirrors before I made my purchase. I chose the best of the lot, but I heard and saw things in all of them."

MATHILDE TSKED WHEN we told her about the mirror, "I'm calling in Fletcher to investigate the suite. I'll have my staff prepare another room for Shelton."

"Investigate?" Damien laughed. "Isn't that a conflict of interest? He's one of the chief suspects."

Mathilde shook her head. "Not everyone is a black magician like you and your ruthless rivals, Damien."

Damien snorted. "It's not as if I'm the only one in the Trade with 'ruthless rivals'. There's a lot of sabotage and cattiness among enchantresses."

I held up the appointment book. "Someone doesn't want my author's trick to expose them. That's why they shattered the mirror. It makes the people in this book suspects."

Crystal frowned. "But you don't know their names until you've had time to review the notes."

"We need to get a new scrying mirror and ear horn, so we can carry on." Damien said.

Crystal said. "I have a scrying bowl I can fill with spring water. Can you make that work?"

I frowned. I'd heard that scrying bowls were a "poor man's divination tool. "I've never used scrying bowls before."

Damien grimaced. "He gets adequate performance from basic magical tools. Though there are some things that work better for him than others."

Crystal raised a brow at this.

"Why does everyone act like this makes me a grand master? Getting the Emporium's cheap products to work isn't a significant accomplishment. Though its magical cleaning tools are useful."

Mathilde bit her lip. "Hm."

Crystal laughed, "Getting a scrying bowl to work should pose no problems for you then."

"I take a while to learn how to use a new tool. I can't guarantee you'll be satisfied with the results."

"We need to try it out at least."

UNFORTUNATELY, WE COULDN'T keep our plan secret from Fletcher. He insisted on being present when I tried using the scrying bowl.

"The Watchers have assigned me to investigate your angel investor. I shouldn't be left out when you hire a consultant."

Damien negotiated terms before he allowed Fletcher into the room.

"I'm willing to keep this private. Making Shelton Sharpe's abilities well known would expose an informant. It may even be preferable to let the Trade think Shelton's author's voice trick was only the result of the mirror."

The scrying bowl was wooden and gilded with silver. They poured fresh spring water into it. I unfolded a letter from a packet Crystal had prepared for me.

The voice was loathsome. "A saucy wench like you deserves only the best. I'm willing to help you trade up from Mathilde Kildare's theater. Let me sponsor you. You won't regret it."

The water was befouled with a visage even more unsavory than the voice. A drooling idiot appeared in the suddenly murky depths. Such a creature was too seedy to fulfill the promises he made to Crystal.

Damien frowned when I wrinkled my nose. I threw the paper down.

"Doesn't it work?"

I tapped the letter. "Don't bother responding to this one. He's a low class creep who's lying about his credentials. He can't even afford a proper wardrobe and hygiene, much less support anyone else."

Fletcher frowned and gestured to the bowl. "There's nothing there!"

I glanced at the visage. "I see a face in the water and I hear the man's voice."

"How do we know you aren't imagining things or lying if we can't see anything ourselves?"

Damien's back bristled at this and the air became so heated by his temper that steam arose from the water. "The scrying mirror and its ear horn made his visions visible and audible to everyone else."

I winced when the vision disappeared, and I just saw my reflection in the bowl. "The vision's gone for me now."

Crystal brought her finger up to her chin. "What about a crystal ball?"

"I've got one I use for decoration. I can get visions when I clean it, but it keeps getting too murky for me to use". I said.

Damien laughed. "That's because it's a lightside trick, and it's too pernicky to work with the darker magics. You're lucky it doesn't turn pitch black."

Crystal smirked. "I'm not a prissy lightsider either. I have to use tools that don't balk at coming into contact with the stronger passions."

She rang a house bell and sent for her crystal ball. The house staff brought it within 15 minutes. It was in a black velvet bag and turned out to be red with lusts, passions, and rages. My intuition often gave me tactile sensations to tell me when I was around a magical object. I gauged their strength and potency by touch, and I used it to buy unsorted spell ingredients in bulk. I placed a finger to it and felt it was as warm as a heart that pulsed with hot-blooded passions yet wasn't consumed by them.

"Well?" Damien asked.

I used a handkerchief to rub off the smudge of the fingerprints I left on it and nodded, "It'll do."

MATHILDE STILL WANTED me to go through the private sessions, so I set up the crystal ball and its cradle in front of me at a table the next morning. Then I worked on the letters the Diamonds had received.

Damien grunted "good" when he could see the letter writers rendered in shades of red. Billy made sketches of what we saw in the ball.

I heard a coarse and crude remark about the first recipient of the letter. I wrinkled my nose when I heard them. "I figure these are low-hanging fruit."

Mathilde took one letter and frowned at its contents. "A stern talking to by a Watcher ought to make him see sense."

Fletcher took the letter and nodded agreement. "They'll receive warnings that petty harassment of the Diamonds won't be tolerated."

Billy spoke up about one letter, "I know this man's name."

"Then write it down for the Watcher."

Billy took out a sheet from his sketchpad and wrote the name down.

He kept this up every time he recognized a letter writer when their face appeared in the crystal ball. Some names came up more than once.

Mathilde's brows rose at this, and she glared at the visages of the cads in the crystal ball.

It surprised me to see some familiar faces from Beldon's Gentleman's Club. Damien made me frequent the place for business networking. He laughed when he saw them appear as I read out the Diamonds' letters.

Fletcher yawned. "How many is left?"

I counted them. "There's 10. They're all Crystal's."

"That's the price Crystal pays for being so popular. I can at least move them off the board for her. We can finish up tomorrow." He took Billy's list of names and called it a night.

Chapter 5-The Menial Minion

Fletcher turned out to be useful. He found out a housemaid named Stella was the last one around the mirror and brought her to us.

Stella cast her gaze down and whispered. "I meant to polish the mirror for tomorrow's interviews, but it broke on me."

"So you're saying it was an accident?" I asked her.

She whimpered "yes" in response. Stella held up a wand I recognized.

"It's a turbo cleaning wand from Quinn's Emporium." They looked at me in surprise. "You should only use the turbo wand in industrial environments."

Damien bit his lip at this while most of the room raised their brows at my statement. I didn't care if my firsthand knowledge was unbecoming for a magician's apprentice. It wasn't my fault Damien forced me to use such tools.

Mathilde sighed and spoke to Stella. "So you used an overpowered wand for cleaning tasks."

She blushed. "We're under new management and were issued new cleaning wands for our work."

"Can I look at it?" They made the wand of tarnished silver. It felt grimy in my hand. Though that was my intuition picking up extra impressions rather than its sloppiness.

"It was nice and shiny when I first started, but got tarnished fast. No amount of silver polish can buff it." Stella said.

"Put the wand under running water. The tarnish is caused by accumulated bad energy. The water will dispel it." I did the same to my cleaning wand every other day.

Mathilde sighed. "They should've given you proper training before you wielded the wand."

Stella whimpered. "I can show you how it's done." I said.

"That's hardly necessary for a guest," Mathilde said.

My intuition said otherwise. "I insist," I said.

THE DIAMOND PALACE accommodated its guests, so they allowed me to take Stella to the kitchens. We went to the sink, and I pumped water over the wand. The runoff turned pitch black at first, but the water became clearer the longer I pumped the water over it. Soon the water was clear, and the wand became radiant. Stella reached in and picked it up in wonder. "I'm glad to be of service to you, but it's not as if it's Merlin's magical staff." I told her.

"I heard you were once a minion, but didn't believe it," she said. Her voice was less hesitant now that we were away from the guests and her employers.

"Yes, I was." There was no reason to say more. My initiation into the Trade wasn't pleasant, and I'd rather not dwell on it.

Her eyes lit up. "That would mean you're the only minion that worked their way up to apprenticeship in decades."

The light of ambition in her eyes caused a frisson of distaste in my spine. It wasn't a matter of caste for me. The sight of ambition in any magic user unnerved me. My master, Damien Rathschild was the most ambitious man I knew in the Trade. It made him the most demanding employer I ever had.

She laughed. "At least the only non-enchantress that's traded up. There's always a market for fresh talent if you've got good glamour.

I shuddered at the inference. The demand for "fresh talent" was ferocious in the Underworld and the Trade. "I can imagine," I said aloud to her.

"How d'you do it?" She asked.

I smiled at her. "That entails trade secrets I'm not free to divulge."

She bit her lower lip at this. "At least Maximus shares what he knows with up-and-comers if you're unwilling to help me."

Which brought to mind the obvious question: who was "Maximus?"

WHEN I CAME BACK TO the main areas Fletcher saw malice in Stella's damage to my property. Mathilde was determined to continue the weekend's social event no matter what. She required me to appear at the consultation sessions.

"It's not good to have too many minions around. There's a lot of cattiness and infighting among them," Fletcher told me.

Mathilde sighed as she waved her fan. "They say the same for junior enchantresses."

I shrugged. "I'm an apprentice now."

"Seeing someone else succeed when they can't makes it even worse for them." Fletcher grumbled.

I glanced at Damien, who nodded agreement to Fletcher's words. "There are petty people who sabotage their betters."

"Humph." I couldn't imagine my master shielding me from said pettiness. "Well it's petty ante compared to the magical battles I've seen."

My words caused in-drawn breaths and a moment of awkward silence. Mathilde glanced at Damien with a furrowed brow.

Damien smirked and took a long swallow of port. "At least you can escalate matters if you need to, Shelton. You can't show clemency to this 'Stella' lest she mistakes it for weakness".

I shuddered under the inference that I'd be expected to do so. Damien was a believer in "consequences" and "object lessons".

"I'll just send a bill to Menials & Minions to cover the damages," I shrugged. "Having her wages garnished should be enough of a rebuke.," Damien nodded at this.

I gave a sigh of relief that I wasn't required to turn this into a vendetta.

Crystal frowned. "Menials & Minions? Stella works for Menials & Minions?"

"That's her employment agency," I said.

"I want her turned out immediately," Crystal said.

"That's rather extreme," Mathilde said.

"I've been receiving notes. They show my movements have been monitored by a so-called admirer. I don't want his informer to continue working here."

"You need proof that Stella is an informer. Otherwise, I won't void her employment contract," Mathilde said.

Crystal looked at Fletcher. "I believe the laying of hex links is enough to warrant an investigation."

She gestured to me. "Stella's committed acts of vandalism against someone that's advanced above her. Is it hard to believe she's done the same with me?"

"I need more to justify a subpoena." Fletcher said.

Which is why Crystal tapped me on the shoulder. "Can I speak to you in private?"

Fletcher smirked at this. But I knew I wasn't being granted a favor but a commission. It wasn't as if I were a master or watcher that caught women's eyes. Women only sought me out for business reasons.

"We can discuss it later. My weekend is booked up."

I CHECKED THE STATUS of my room. Stella was there. She still wore a maid's uniform, but it was so low cut it looked like she wanted to compete with Mathilde's Diamonds.

A modest diamond pendant was nestled in the hollow between her breasts. "The only way you could afford that is if you got a patron to give you an overgenerous tip."

She gave me a knowing smile when I looked at her too long. "I wanted to compensate you for your shattered mirror."

She took a deep breath waiting for my response, and it expanded her cleavage.

"I see. You're offering payment in trade."

Stella smirked agreement.

"I could never understand that fantasy. It's bad taste to molest the help when they're just trying to do their jobs."

Kirkton Academy was a church run on-site school of an orphanage. Many of their female graduates had that happen to them when they entered service. Stella was willing. However, the memory of my fellow graduates spoiled the effect.

Her brows came together at first. "You really were a minion, weren't you?"

She took out a calling card from her cleavage. "Perhaps this is more to your liking. I moonlight as a hostess at the Hellfire Club."

I smiled at her. "That sounds like something an enchantress would do."

She shrugged in a way that squeezed her breasts together. "I'm looking to work my way up to my dream job."

I chuckled as she left the room.

STELLA SERVED AS LIVING proof I'd gained a preference for women without glamour. Now that I was in the Trade, my knowledge of its day-to-day reality destroyed the mystique.

My master enjoyed being around the glamorous, but I was the one who got assigned the tasks he agreed to do for them. He was generous with my time and services. The closest I came to enjoying them was when I charged a fee they had to pay.

Crystal invited the both of us to a business meeting in one of the Diamond Palace's private rooms that night. A woman from Quality would've insisted on chaperons. However, I knew enough about the Trade not to have salacious expectations.

She was dressed in an evening gown as she made her appeal and paced the floor in high-heeled slippers. The bottom of her dress was cut to show their elegance. It was considered more scandalous than the low cut of her gown bodice. Though I couldn't understand Quality's preoccupation with ankles.

"Fletcher refuses to deal with this man for me," she said.

"He found letters from him in Stella's room but gave her a warning." Crystal shook with rage. "She's convinced she thought she was only delivering the notes from one of my admirers. As if it was a harmless sideline, and she didn't realize they were distressing to me."

"It won't be the first time the help's had a sideline," I shrugged. Maximus wasn't the first one who paid for services from an underling. I had done so myself in pursuit of one of my Master's objectives.

She glared at me. "Why do all the men believe her? She hasn't even got glamour."

"Some women do well without it," I shrugged.

Damien laughed. "Shelton allowed his better judgment to be swayed. That's the biggest compliment Shelton can give a woman. He's not usually so credulous with anyone."

Crystal took a deep breath. "How can you believe her, after she vandalized your mirror to keep the author of my notes from being seen? You can't tell me she didn't realize the notes were 'upsetting'. Not when she went to great efforts to protect their author."

The room fell silent as I considered this. I'm not oblivious to women, but I accepted the fact my blood ran cooler than other men's. "That's not something I thought of."

"I expect you to get back up to form and take care of the man harassing me."

My brows rose. "Take care of him?"

She rolled her eyes at this. "Nothing extreme. Just find some leverage I can use to get him to stop harassing me."

"I usually charge a fee for these types of services. I want a retainer-"

Crystal clapped her hands together. "Send the bill to Mathilde. She'll pay for it."

Chapter 6-A Cease and Desist Letter

When Fletcher left the room, Damien spoke. "Carry on, Shelton."

Mathilde's brows rose. "Is that wise?"

Damien gestured to the door where Fletcher departed the room. "He's good enough to intimidate the low-hanging fruit. However, I prefer to deal with the more challenging suspects themselves."

Crystal rubbed the goosebumps on her forearms as I read over the letter. "We've missed you at the Club." A voice cackled.

A man of saturnine aspect appeared in the ball and Crystal snorted. He had black locks and piercing black eyes with a closely clipped mustache and goatee. "Samuel Covington was the manager there, but he worked under the club's owner."

"Hmm," Damien said, suddenly alert. "Maximus's known for poaching the most promising dark arts apprentices." Of course, I'd never heard of him. I just got into the Trade the year before and had no magical talents before the infusion ritual Damien used on me.

"Does the note have an address?"

I turned it over. "All it has is a flame sigil."

Damien sighed.

I tapped the sigil, and it jarred a memory for Crystal. "The Hellfire Club is very exclusive. They customize their codewords for each prospect. Recruitment was part of the job description. Promising novices were preferred." Crystal nodded.

Damien sniffed. "What you need is a good employment lawyer not a besotted champion."

"You are so clever," Mathilde said with a smile as she placed a finger on his hand

Damien rolled his eyes. "I'd prefer an honest trade between us at a set rate. Not a woman who uses her allure as an extortion scheme. I suggest you find a lawyer and pay his regular rate with money and not trade. You need his wits to be sharp and not befuddled by glamour.

The women's mouths gaped open at Damien's words, but I agreed with him. It wasn't as if they were Ladies of Quality and had to be ignorant of good business practices."

Damien nodded. "I made a sketch of the sender." Damien showed them his sketch. I showed they matched the author of the notes with the crystal ball.

The women's eyes lit with recognition. Mathilde made a hissing intake of breath. "Maximus Worthington."

Damien nodded, "Good, we can give Fletcher a clear target."

FLETCHER FROWNED AT the sketch of the man's face. "The letters are unsigned. Maximus Worthington has high standing in the Trade. Accusing him of writing them because of an uncertified handwriting expert is unlawful." Fletcher said as he looked over the sketch.

Damien's eyes narrowed at this. He'd based some retaliatory strikes to death threats on my author's voice trick. Though he didn't mention this when he spoke. "I've run my own tests. He's accurate."

Fletcher sighed. "You're not an unbiased proctor, and you're in conflict of interest."

"Why don't we run our own tests to see how accurate Mr. Sharpe's ability is"? Crystal asked.

"It won't be admissible in a court of law." Fletcher said.

Mathilde spoke up. "But we can see if this is an avenue worth pursuing. I'll pay for his certification exam if he passes our private tests."

THE DIAMONDS HAD PLENTY of anonymous notes to test me with. Cards that had been left with gifts. Addresses and times written without names.

Ruby placed a card before me. "This was left unsigned, but I know who wrote it."

I took the card and heard the words. "Come to me in the park at midnight."

A man's face appeared. It was some bohemian with a frowzy linen shirt he left unbuttoned.

Ruby nodded "yes" at this. "That's the One." She stared into the mirror for a long second. Then took back the card.

Fletcher rolled his eyes. "Let's do a blind test. We'll all write on a card and not sign it. Let's see if he can decipher the letter writer."

Mathilde, Crystal, and Ruby wrote on slips of notepaper. They folded the papers in half and put the slips in a bowl. Once the slips were collected Mathilde shook the bowl, so they jumbled the slips up.

I took the slips out. They'd written their names, but the voices I heard didn't match names on the slips. I read out the names and spoke the author's voices. The crystal flickered the authors' images as I called them out.

"Mathilde wrote 'Crystal Moore.' Crystal wrote 'Ruby Reed.' Ruby wrote 'Mathilde Kildaire'". The younger women squealed in delight each time I got the author's name right.

"That's three for three," Mathilde grinned.

Fletcher brows came together. "Humph, I've seen nothing like this. The Watcher's Tribunal will run more vigorous tests, though. He doesn't qualify as an expert witness yet."

"I'm not a charlatan, but my abilities don't make me a great magician." I shrugged, wondering when this night would end, and I could end this performance.

Crystal laughed, "I've seen too many prodigies burn out. This is a useful service and a valid contribution to the Trade. You can base your entire career on this ability alone."

"That's good to know," I said as I took some apple juice from the refreshment table

"I trust my apprentice has proven himself," Damien said.

Fletcher grunted "yes".

"At least we know it's worth investigating Maximus Worthington about my anonymous notes." Crystal said.

"We still need to get Shelton Sharpe certified before the Watchers can sign a subpoena for Maximus."

Crystal pouted, "What would it take to get Shelton Sharpe certified?"

"We'll take care of that in time." Mathilde sighed. "As it is, I have a signed sample of Maximus's writing I collected before I retired. We can compare the two."

Fletcher nodded. "Good, we can use a certified analyst to analyze it."

"Wait here. I must retrieve it myself." Mathilde said. She was gone for a long moment before she came back with a lacquer box. It had a mother-of-pearl and golden heart inlaid on it.

"Maximus managed enchantresses before he became a patron. He had a gift for forming connexions in the theater world. Unfortunately, he got possessive of me. He told prospective patrons I was already taken when they made me offers." Mathilde said.

Damien rolled his eyes." I think I remember him."

I frowned. Damien would've been young when Mathilde was in her prime. It was strange for him to have known her that long. They may be "old friends" but I didn't think that meant they were that old.

Mathilde sighed. "Yes, he was even possessive about you, and told me to send you to boarding school to keep you out of sight from my admirers."

Damien bit his lip as if he didn't like this slip.

She opened the box and found it empty. Mathilde hissed at this. "I'm dismissing that creature. This isn't just an honest mistake. This is willful theft."

She ran a bell to summon Stella, but there was no answer.

"I can't believe this. She ran off with the only signed handwriting sample we had," Crystal fumed.

Damien spoke. "There may be another." He turned to Mathilde, "Didn't you dismiss him when you found he had another enchantress on his string? Perhaps they have an example we can use?"

Fletcher sighed. "I'm willing to do a follow-up if you find a signed handwriting sample. I'll take the unsigned notes in the meantime."

"I'll go get them," Crystal said, and he left the room with her.

As soon as they were out Damien said, "I'd like to speak to you in private, Mathilde."

Mathilde sighed, "Ruby is my designated successor. Whatever you say to me, you can say to her."

"Very well then, Mathilde. It would be much simpler if you let me use the curse as a link."

Ruby's eyes widened at this while Mathilde said. "I only want that done as a last resort, Damien."

"Then I propose a gentler means that may be more to your liking."

Damien pointed at me. "You haven't objected to Shelton sending past due notices for you. They have a built-in jinx that is triggered if the payment isn't made. We can have him craft a notice to Maximus that he is to send the contract back to us."

"He's the one who writes the past due notices?" Mathilde asked as if it were a wonder instead of the monetization of a modest talent. My jinxes faded fast and were a light version of the hexes Damien preferred.

"I haven't been able to work him up to hexes yet, but he's good at light but effective touches." Damien said.

Ruby laughed, "The past due notices are effective enough for my liking. Your apprentice has skills." She must've seen more impressive talents in her time, and it was strange to hear such praise.

"There's people who dread the notices more than a death curse," Mathilde said. "You have my permission to craft such a letter. I'd like to see it before the end of this weekend and have it posted on Monday."

"I must go home and get my special ink for the letter." I said.

"Do you mean Quinn Emporium sells jinxed ink? Perhaps I could write the letter myself." Mathilde asked.

"No, the ink is a potion that has special ingredients to act as a carrier for his jinxes." Damien said. "The ink helps convey the jinx, but it'd be useless to you if you don't have the ability yourself."

Ruby nodded at this. "It'd be best to leave Fletcher out of this. Affixing a jinx to the letter is a gray area."

I SPENT THE REST OF the evening acting as a scribe for Mathilde as she debated the precise wording of the letter.

This is what we came up with:

Mister Maximus Worthington,

I am Shelton Sharpe. I am writing on behalf of Mathilde Kildaire, the proprietress of The Diamond Palace.

It has come to our attention that you hold an employment contract for Miss Crystal Moore. You claim she is still beholden to you yet, she was dismissed from your establishment.

According to the Trade's employment laws, apprenticeships are only valid for seven years. They are never perpetual. Miss Moore has been working for us for seven years and any employment contract you have with her is no longer valid. Therefore, we request you give up the contract for review. Otherwise, our legal advisors will file a motion to dismiss your claims on her services.

You have 30 days to comply with this request.

Signed

Shelton Sharpe for Mathilde Kildaire, The Diamond Palace.

"That should be good enough.

Shelton will write it out in his special ink and apply the jinx to it." Damien said as he read it out.

"What happens if Maximus refuses the letter?" Ruby asked.

"Then the jinx will be triggered sooner," Damien shrugged. "I made Shelton add this refinement to my past due notices."

It'd taken two months to add this "refinement" to the past due notices I wrote. We knew it worked when there was notice of a house fire caused when a recipient tried to burn the letter. Damien had made me clip out the article for his scrapbook.

Chapter 7-The Letter is Returned

Once we returned home, I had to rewrite out the message with the special ink we brewed for my jinxes. It had certain additives my jinx could latch on to and transferred it to the page.

Maximus would have a reasonable timeframe to grant our request. However, our patience wasn't limitless. I had enough of a spine to set this boundary, at least.

"I wish Mathilde would let me take stronger measures with Maximus." Damien said as he looked over the letter before affixing his sigil to it.

"Of course, she's near a Watcher. She needs to make the effort at a peaceful negotiation for appearances' sake. Consulting with me is a big step for her. She doesn't approve of my profession."

I glanced at him. Mathilde struck me as respectable. You'd think she'd object to a black magician on principle. It was surprising she hadn't informed on him. So maybe magic had silenced her scruples? Or else yet another woman was swayed by his striking looks, even if she had no hope of gaining his attentions?

He took out his sealing wax and signet ring from his desk. "He'll be less likely to dismiss the letter if he realizes there will be consequences for ignoring us."

The sealing wax was silver, but my jinx turned it a smokey gray as if it were dark magic. He did this for all our final notices. Seeing our magic meld together like this was unnerving, but was a part of my apprenticeship.

THE ANSWER TO OUR LETTER came in the next morning's mail, which was an agreeable surprise.

Tobias saw this while I sorted the morning mail at the breakfast table. He cackled. "That's the fastest turnaround time your letters have ever hand."

"Yes," Damien said with a smirk as he held his hand out for the letter.

And this is why Damien Rathschild is the master. I thought as I handed the envelope over to him. None of my responses were ever this fast.

Damien took out his athame to open the letter. He scowled when he saw its contents. "Is something wrong?"

My cat's fur stood on end, and Scrappy was even more sensitive to my master's moods than I was. The fact Damien scared him was unnerving. Tobias's beak dropped open wordlessly.

He turned the envelope upside down and widened its opening, so the contents fell out onto the table. I winced when I saw my writing. He ripped the letter I wrote in half and returned it to me. "Humph," Damien examined it and pointed to a large red spot on the envelope.

Tobias broke his silence with a titter. "It looks like your letter gave Maximus Worthington a paper cut."

My heart lurched at the thought of my jinx found to be ineffectual.

"Your jinx didn't intimidate him, but he underestimated you." Damien looked me square in the eye, skewering me like a bug under a pin. "It is your job to make him regret that. You need to escalate matters."

"Escalate?".

"You must use the blood from the papercut as a link." Damien tapped the red spot. "He was a fool not to reverse the hex. An imbecile to give us something we can use for blood magic. There's enough here to make a link. Bring me the curry mix."

"Don't you need to apply it to him directly?" The curry mix didn't need magic to inflame flesh with a bad allergic reaction. I had to use it with gloves.

"This blood is a link to Maximus. Applying the curry to the blood spot will affect him physically."

I found the curry powder in the kitchen and brought it out. A little curry could spice a dish. More than that made them inedible. I brought the jar of curry powder and the thin leather gloves to the table as Damien ordered me. "I don't expect you to unleash death curses at this point in your training, but I expect to see progress from you. Put the gloves on and dip a finger in the curry powder."

The operation felt silly, but I followed his orders. "Rub the powder on the spot as if you're rubbing it into his open papercut."

I wrinkled my nose at this. "Wouldn't that aggravate the cut?" That wasn't even ruthless, it was petty.

"That's what you want. You can't reach him so you exorcise your emotions with this ritual."

The ritual would exorcise Damien's tension if not mine own. I was more annoyed at Damien and Crystal than I was at Maximus.

The orange powder became red-orange. "Do it again, that'll only turn his flesh red."

What did he expect me to do with such a petty spell? Give Maximus a rash? I'd want to do more than that if I were to give someone a hex. Such penny ante tricks would make me a bottom-feeder. The curry powder turned brown.

Damien gave me a withering glance, "Again."

When would this be over? Crystal would call me a poor champion when her own protector expected me to do all the work. Let me move on with my life and onto a new assignment rather than be at a spoiled woman's beck and call. I hadn't even wanted this job. It was supposed to be a simple favor, not a chore that didn't end.

Damien smiled when the curry powder turned black. It permeated the air like a pungent dish that had burned. He nodded and said. "Good, it's taken."

I felt drained by the experience. As if I'd embarrassed myself by throwing a petty tantrum over a trifle.

Damien patted me on the shoulder, and I started. "Good, you've laid your first hex on someone."

I glanced at the paper with its black spot.

THE MASTIFF ANNOUNCED a delivery when it came later in the morning. "Come out to the front. You need to sign for a delivery."

Luckily, or not, I was doing the housecleaning at the time, so I was available to sign it. "What do you mean a delivery? I ordered nothing? They better not be charging us for anything?"

This piqued my curiosity, and I went to receive the package. The Mastiff's eyes glowed red. He wasn't glaring at the delivery clerk, but was on high alert. The clerk had a large crate on a dolly. "Sign this please," the clerk said.

I held up a hand to decline the pen. "Not if it means I have to pay upon delivery," I said.

"They prepaid the shipment."

I placed a hand on the crate and found they shielded it, so I couldn't pick up any magical energies from it. Most people didn't know my intuition made me sense magic by touch. Though the Trade's shopkeepers knew I could gauge the potency of spell ingredients.

Screening Damien's death threats made me good at sensing hexes. It wasn't the most grandiose of talents, but Damien told me to keep it a trade secret.

"Well?" the Mastiff asked. It was Damien's ward against hostile magic and good at sensing threats, but he consulted with me too.

"I can't sense anything from them. It looks like they shielded it."

"Don't open it until the Master comes back. You've cast your first hex. This may be Maximus's escalation," the Mastiff said.

My heart rose in my throat. I knew that black magicians feuded among themselves. I'd seen how magicians fought. What he said was likely, though I'd need Damien to confirm things for me.

"SO THE SENDER INSULATED the crate from your intuitive senses?" Damien said.

I nodded "yes."

Damien's brows rose at this. "Would Maximus have learned of your intuition? That you get tactile impressions of the type and potency of magic?"

His piercing look made my heart speed up, and a caused a sheen of sweat to appear on my forehead. I didn't know if it was from my fear or his pyrokenetic abilities. "I've never confessed this ability in public. However, I showed it at the Diamond Palace when my scrying mirror was shattered. There are also some shopkeepers who cater to the Trade that may know about it. They know I have a knack for choosing quality spell ingredients."

Damien sighed, and it felt like a cool breeze dispelled the heat to my senses. "So he might've gathered enough information to make a deduction about your abilities."

He turned his gaze to the crate. "You've started your first feud," Damien smiled as if he was a father who watched his son make his first baby steps.

"What are we to do with the crate? We can't leave it around here."

Damien shrugged. "The Watchers are involved now, so we'll act like respectable practitioners."

My brows came together. "What does that mean?"

"It means we'll report a suspicious delivery and let them analyze and defuse the crate. We'll do this with the same expectation of protection a law-abiding citizen has."

"What about my jinx and hex?" I asked.

He shrugged. "They're nothing but petty mischief. You're a young and promising apprentice. The type the Watcher's Council is prone to indulging. All you'll get is a lecture. They will expect Maximus to adhere to a higher standard as a Master of the Trade. He'll get a harsher reprimand. Fletcher may even get you to lay charges against him."

It was good to hear that I'd earned my fee from Mathilde and done all I would do for her.

Chapter 8-The Black Knight

There was a letter from Menials & Minions in the mail the next morning. I opened it to find a cheque from them.

I placed the letter and cheque on the breakfast table and pushed it over to Damien. "This letter was in the mail."

"At least your jinx got some results. Maximus obviously wants all debts settled between us."

I was glad I wouldn't have to escalate things anymore.

A PACKAGE CAME IN THE mail and I saw it had a woman's rounded writing. I brought it to the breakfast table, assuming it was for Damien.

He shoved it over to me. "It's for you."

It shocked me to see my name on its label instead.

Tobias fluttered his wings in laughter. "For you? Careful, it might be your first hate mail."

I touched the package. "I sense magic but not hostile intent."

My intuition spoke to me in tactile impressions. Anything with black magic gave repugnant frostbite. This package felt cozy and warm.

"Where'd it come from?" There was a sigil of a C monogram inside a diamond on it.

It caught Damien's attention. "Enchantresses send notes instead of gifts. Not unless you're related to them."

I opened it up. There was a note attached to it. *This crystal ball is made from a ruby. It's nothing but a pretty bauble to me. You can put it to better use than I can. Consider it compensation for your damaged scrying mirror.*

Damien ripped open the top to see the red crystal ball. "How touching."

There was more paper in the envelope. I saw it contained a cheque that covered my usual consultant's fee for helping Quality misses. Most times I freed their money from greedy male relatives who were trustees of their funds. Social matrons appreciated my work and recommended me to each other discreetly. I kept up appearances for their sake.

She'd added a time and date for an appointment at a respectable tea room, not an assignation. I often used it as an office for my consultations.

The cheque was the usual fee I demanded for a retainer. It covered a month of services. My cases rarely covered more time than that.

Damien sighed when he saw the cheque. He preferred I work in the Trade. These assignments meant legal and financial maneuvers instead of magic.

"See what she wants. You're to be in her service if it requires only legal and financial maneuverings. She must pay you for more time if she wants you to serve her longer than that."

"MY LETTERS NOW COME from the Hellfire Club. I fear he's sold my contract as a transferable bond." She wrote to me. I assumed this meeting was to hire me to track the contract.

There was a private room in a tea shop whose owner assumed I was more successful with women than I was. I used it to meet my female clients since it'd be awkward for them to come to my home office.

Mrs. Elgin grinned at me, "Maybe this is the one, Mr. Sharpe."

I was lucky she didn't consider my high turnover of companions scandalous. Unless the fact I met women over tea made her assume I was a gentleman?

Crystal looked fetching, and I found her efforts more striking than I had at the Diamond Palace. She appeared to be a pert Quality Miss. Her pale hair was up in a buoyant hair style with becoming ringlet tendrils. I didn't know how she made her cheeks so pink without rouge. Her peaches and cream complexion was radiant.

Her dove gray dress had a high neck, but still encased her perfect figure in well tailored lines. She smirked when I looked at her too long. "You don't enjoy molesting housemaids, so I thought I'd try something different. Some of my patrons like me to play 'the pretty schoolmarm.'"

"You carry the role well." I said. Even if I didn't like having my preferences cataloged by the enchantresses. It was hard to enjoy their charms when they were your potential rivals in the Trade.

I took a seat. "Thank you for the crystal ball. It was a thoughtful gift."

"You need a divination tool that doesn't get fussy about the darker passions yet isn't black magic." She sighed.

"You sound like a patron yourself," I said.

"It's just advice. Rathschild wants you to be a black magician, yet you get results with more discreet methods. The Hellfire Club put up a mist to hide themselves when I sent Fletcher to deliver a warning for me."

Which explained why she hired me. Though I wondered why he didn't use some magic spectacles from Quinn's Emporium. They helped me see past the glamour. It was a simple but effective tool. "So far my skills have been enough." I said.

"Black magicians aren't the only ones that produce thugs. Fletcher beats bad patrons into submission. He's only useful when there's an obvious target. My enemy hides in the shadows."

"So you want me to be your protector?" I asked.

"Fletcher is my protector. What I want you to do is give him something to aim for. I don't see you as a weakling, but you're not a shock trooper to send against my enemies."

"We got a clear view of the letter writer at the palace," I said.

"Maximus makes other men do his dirty work. His underlings might have records, but Maximus doesn't. Fletcher needs more than your visions to arrest him."

I looked at her. "Do you want Maximus cursed?"

She laughed at this. "And I was told you were a smart one. You're willing to curse him without doing any reconnaissance? He's likely a master himself."

"Or a poseur." I shrugged. He couldn't be impressive if he got an allergic reaction through my hex on the blood droplet.

"A poseur who's got a group of novices following him."

I frowned. "You mean he gets responses to his business cards? I assumed they were junk mail for seedy establishments."

She laughed at this. "So he's sent you invitations?"

I nodded "yes." "He approached me by one of his recruiters, though the offer may be rescinded by now. My name's on the letter I sent for Mathilde."

Crystal blinked, either to hold back tears or to bat her lashes at me. "I need more than a cease and desist letter. He's more likely to leave me alone if he thinks I have a protector from a practitioner of the Dark Arts. Either out of fear or professional courtesy. I'm willing to pay you to create this impression for me. You don't have to be my champion."

Creating such an impression was no worse than the petty cons I used to run before I joined the Trade. I nodded "yes". "Delivering an in-person cease and desist order at the Hellfire Club shouldn't require too much from me. Your current retainer should cover the time and expense of executing this ploy for you. You must pay me more if you want me to do more."

She nodded at this. "I prefer paying a set rate too, rather than being expected to be forever grateful and eternally in debt. That's what got me in trouble with Maximus."

Crystal continued. "Your plan sounds splendid. We enchantresses are supposed to be discreet about our affairs. Maximus won't expect us to maintain an elaborate spectacle of ourselves. A simple countermeasure could take the pressure off me."

"So, it's settled. I will go to the Hellfire Club to warn Maximus Worthington away from you?"

She nodded "yes" at this.

I ASSUMED AN OUTING at the Hellfire Club would be no worse than any other after work hours' entertainment. Damien didn't care what I did at night. Though I must be awake and alert on the job in the daytime.

I had a mourning suit I used to attend funerals. I'd never had to attend one for someone I mourned. Damien used these events as social occasions. It occurred to me that black would be an excellent choice for the Hellfire Club.

Tobias caught me before I headed out. "Did someone you know die?"

"It's work related." I said.

"The Master is staying in tonight." Tobias said. I usually attended funerals with him.

"I'm visiting the Hellfire Club for a paid assignment." Tobias didn't allow me to say more than that.

"Wait here." He said before he flew off.

Damien came to the front a moment later, frowning. He had my spectacles in his hand.

I waved it away. "That won't fool anyone."

"But it'll be easier to overlook you. The Trade doesn't mind you slumming as long as you take the effort to be discreet." He said.

I sighed and put the spectacles on. They made me look 30 years older.

"What are you planning to do?"

"I'm going down there to warn them away from Crystal and let them think I'm her protector." I shrugged.

"Weren't they the ones who shattered the scrying mirror?"

"They paid for the damages. Crystal gave me a replacement. I got an invitation to the club I can use from Stella."

Damien nodded. "It's good they want to recruit you. You won't face a hostile coven. I suggest you make your 'warning' a request. Don't get obsequious but make it sound like a minor favor you want from the club. They're more likely to honor that than an open challenge."

"I won't commit to anything if I don't have to."

Damien grinned, "You're capable of remaining civil but uncommitted. They'll want more from you, of course. Though you can convince them it's better to remain on good terms with you rather than making you an enemy."

I snorted. "I almost wish I could bellow out threats like Fletcher would."

"Crystal would've sent Fletcher if that's what she wanted. Hopefully this brief excursion will be the end of it. I don't like you being distracted. Especially since Stella works at the club."

"I've never been a gallant. Crystal's paid me for my time. I won't do anything beyond it."

THE CARD HAD AN ADDRESS that included a set of directions. It told me to "follow the ley line in the East End" to get to 666 Helios Street. This would've confused a non-magician. My intuition made me so prickly I avoided ley lines.

In this case, the goosebumps on my flesh penetrated me to the marrow and gave me pinpricks on the mind. I was used to Damien's discretion and wondered why the Watchers hadn't shut this place down. But the fact the Hellfire Club was in the Hallows probably confused things.

A blunderer would assume the unease they sensed was from being in a dangerous neighborhood. They wouldn't know it was from black magic. I paused when the ley line lead to a dark alley that could be used as a trap by a mugger. A gas lamp lit up to encourage me to enter it. The alley was now a brightly lit narrow stairway.

At least they kept it clean. If only because there'd be no place to walk if otherwise. I took a deep breath and walked into the stairway. It was like entering an underworld.

There was a gargoyle faced doorknocker, and I used it. The doorkeeper opened a small window to look at me.

"Humph." I thought the snort meant they would deny me entrance, but the door opened.

"And you're supposed to be the top novice in the Trade? I wouldn't expect such penny ante glamour from you." The man muttered. He held a picture of me clipped from a Warlock's Weekly article.

"There's not much sense wasting energy when a simple spell will work for camouflage." I shrugged.

I took off the spectacles and put them in my pocket, so they could see me without the aging glamour.

He nodded at this. "It'll take more than simple tricks to impress the regulars around here. But it may be smart to save your firepower for later."

Chapter 9-Delivering A Warning

"I thought this was a gentleman's club for gathering connexions in the Trade." I said. Hoping my appeal for clarification could stare this conversation into civil territory.

The doorman smirked, "You have to prove your worth associating with to form a connexion here."

A man on a couch grunted at this.

"You booted Harry from Warlock Weekly's number one spot. He's been wanting to test your mettle since then." The doorman grinned.

I looked at him. "So this is an ambush."

A young man walked up to us and smiled. He had a clipboard in hand and put a check mark next to my name on it. "This is an initiation for new pledges. We have a multi-step screening process. Getting within the top three spots on Warlock Weekly's Top 10 List is only the first step."

"I see."

Harry got up and walked towards me. "You didn't bring your wand here."

"I was told I wasn't to bring any to social occasions as a courtesy."

Harry snorted at this. "Yet, you brought magical spectacles, which shows this isn't a social occasion for you."

I held up the pair. "The Hellfire Club isn't a high society cotillion. This accessory doesn't have offensive capabilities. I'm told young gentlemen have to be 'discreet.' I assume the use of camouflage isn't a sign of hostile intent, even if it's not 'honorable.'"

He blinked his eyes and grunted as he tried to digest my words and then shook his head. "Listening to you is as bad as listening to Maximus. You talk too fast for me to make out what you're saying."

"I have to be fast to work with my master."

"Who's that?" He sniffed.

"Damien Rathschild."

Everyone grunted, "Of course."

A young woman walked up to me with a smile. It was Stella. Her uniform was low cut in the bodice and the skirt. She was pretty, but her makeup was garish. "This is Stella. You'll be seeing a lot of her I trust."

The doorman pointed to himself. "I'm Edgar."

Then he pointed to the one with a clipboard. "Orion keeps us organized."

Stella had to be more sedate at the Diamond Palace. Her appearance at the Hellfire Club was at the other extreme in the saucy maid outfit. The sight of a wand in her hands made me think she was a club member. I assume they wouldn't allow eye candy to be armed.

"This is a coed club?" I said, gesturing to Stella.

"Stella is our top hostess," Edgar said.

No wonder why Crystal didn't want to return to this club. So far, I didn't see signs anyone was too boorish here. Though why should she be a glorified waitress instead of a premiere enchantress?

"I believe I saw one of your hostesses at the Diamond Palace."

Stella kept the professional smile on her face, but her eyes lit up at my words.

"Some prefer to forget where they came from," Orion said.

"Apprentices only have to serve their masters for seven years. Are hostesses indentured like minions are?"

Stella spoke up, "No, the establishments prefer to see fresh faces and have a high turnover. They're released once they stop drawing crowds."

My brows creeped up at this. "Then what's the harm in leaving your audience wanting more and moving on?"

"The anti-competition clause says differently." Harry grunted.

Stella sighed at this.

"Is there a 'anti-competition clause' for club members too?"

"Things are different for club members. There's an entrance exam to get into the Club and only one spot available. We're competing for the spot" Harry added.

"I see." I said.

Of course, it wasn't a written exam like Josiah Nesfer had given me.

Harry pointed to two straw dummies in the left corner of the room with bulls-eyes on their chests.

"First one to destroy them wins. Mine's on the left. Yours is on the right."

Stella counted down, "At the count of five. One, two, three, four, five."

He fired off a firebolt from his wand. All I could do was yell, "jinx" at the shot. His bolt curved to the right and hit mine.

It left a scorch mark at the bullseye, and the scent of hay was like incense.

"You're supposed to hit yours, not his." Stella said to Harry.

Harry turned red and fired five in rapid succession while I chanted "jinx." Each and every bolt would've incinerated me in a duel. However, they missed his dummy and landed on mine until it was reduced to sooty ashes. His own dummy was untouched.

He huffed and puffed from the exertion. His face flushed so red I thought he'd pass out from heatstroke. His eyes were bloodshot.

My heart raced. I hadn't meant to give him an injury.

Stella gave him some water from off a nearby tray. "You need to relax, Harry, and cool down. You're in danger of spontaneous combustion at this rate."

Harry grunted at this and accepted the drink. "Can you give me some beer instead?"

She sighed. "You're an inflamed pyrokenetic. It won't be safe to give you anything combustible until you've cooled down. I'll wait until your color goes back to normal."

He drank from his glass and accepted more glasses from her without any more comments.

Stella's efforts were accepted without comment. It made me understood 'hostessing' was more complicated than looking pretty.

Orion and Edgar debated my admission into the club all the while. They inspected the straw dummies critically.

"Harry's dummy is untouched though he decimated Shelton's dummy." Frederick wrote on his clipboard.

"All the firepower in the world doesn't help you if you can't shoot straight." Owen snorted.

"He was jinxed. It affected his aim." Frederick said.

"We need to see how he aims when he isn't jinxed."

They turned to face me. "How long do your jinxes last?"

I shrugged. "Until my objective is reached."

"But it must have a shelf life?"

I opened my mouth and was at a loss for words for a moment. "That's something I'd need to research. But I never claimed I could lay a curse that would last for generations."

Orion raised his brows. "At least not yet. Working under Rathschild should help you foment the rage you need to turn a hex into a curse."

Stella spoke from the couch. "You conserved your energy by laying a simple hex. Perhaps a simple counter would do?"

"Simple counter?" Harry asked.

"Has anyone got one of Quinn's rabbit foots?"

Harry snorted. "I practice my shots every day. This gives me skill. I don't need luck."

"Under normal circumstances, but it may counter Shelton's jinx?"

Edgar went to a box and took out a complimentary rabbit's foot.

It was snow-white at first but became smoky grey when Harry took it in his hands.

Orion said. "Try shooting your dummy now."

Harry got up and stood in front of his dummy. He fired a huge firebolt that incinerated the dummy.

He smirked and waved his wand dismissively. "He can't be so tough if a simple counter works against him."

I spoke up when I saw where this was heading. "There was no use wasting my energy for a friendly competition. The hex would've been stronger if this were a life or death struggle."

He humphed but didn't have a quick reply ready. Indeed, he now looked pale and exhausted. Stella called out to a server. "Bring me some juice."

The juice came on a tray, and she presented it to Harry with a pretty smile. He accepted it and drank. His face regained its color.

Orion and Edgar both nodded. "Conserving energy until you need it is a sound combat strategy."

"Does Maximus insist pledges fight each other to death?" I asked. "Do you want this challenge to continue?"

Harry frowned. I didn't want to press my advantage, but Maximus may not give me much choice."

Orion smiled. "I can see why you're the top novice in the Trade."

"It's a tough call. Harry has more firepower. Shelton's jinxes are subtle but effective." Frederick said.

"Of course, there are times when we itch to blast our opponents to ashes. However, sometimes we need to undermine someone who's too highly placed to attack directly. Both could be useful to the Club. We must leave the final choice to Maximus," Edgar said.

I played the part of an interested prospect who wanted to make an informed choice. "I'm interested in forming connexions at this club. But I'm told they don't allow people to move on when they need to advance in their studies."

Edgar sniffed. "Crystal Moore likes to trade up. Her ambition means she has a high turnover in protectors. She'll burn out every bridge at the rate she's going."

I laughed at this. "We're dark practitioners. It's a part of our Trade."

Stella said nothing, but nodded "yes" at this.

I shrugged off the innuendo. "Starting at the bottom shouldn't mean you're forced to stay there. I started as a minion myself, and now I'm the top apprentice in the Trade. Crystal feels no guilt in working her way up to a more upscale venue. She feels she paid her way while she was here and owes her former employer nothing. I agree with her."

Stella's mouth fell open in an "ooh" as if I made some grand proclamation of love for Crystal.

Edgar, Orion, and Harry's nostrils flared at my words. They were so shocked at what I said, I walked out without incident.

I'd made an effective show of strength. It should convince them Crystal had an able protector to speak for her rights. Such ploys were commonplace in the Trade.

THE HELLFIRE CLUB HAD the gall to send me an invitation to "discuss this matter with us." I ignored it but there was a write-up about our dispute in Warlock's Weekly.

Damien snorted at the letter they wrote. "It'd be foolish to let yourself go to a place where you'd be outnumbered. Yet, they'll make you sound cowardly if you refuse this offer."

I took the paper and read it. "If they want to challenge me in the open. Then we'll negotiate in the open."

I went to my office and wrote a response. *I'd prefer to meet Maximus Worthington on neutral ground for negotiations.* Then I mailed the letter to Warlock Weekly's offices.

Let the onus of cowardice be on them if they refused a reasonable request such as this.

Warlock's Weekly couldn't resist getting involved. The editor gave a comment when they printed my letter: *We'd be willing to rent the Watchers Hall to host such an event.*

Chapter 10-The Premier Apprentice in the Trade

The Hellfire Club wouldn't have been impressed if they saw me using a wand to do the housework again. However, I had to return to my routine once I delivered my message for Crystal.

There was a write-up on the entrance exam in the Warlock Weekly's editorial. Damien read it out to me as I served him and the familiars' breakfasts.

Shelton Sharpe won the duel with Harry Hardwick. That means I'm forced to name him the premiere apprentice in the Trade for the second week in a row. I say 'forced' because he used a cheap jinxing trick to affect Harry's aim in the contest. That's something that that anyone can use a rabbit's foot from Quinn's Emporium to counter.

Mr. Sharpe won't be able to keep his position or his prize if he doesn't display some serious firepower.

I snorted. "I suppose the only power he recognizes is 'firepower'? He regards anything else as 'treachery.'"

I'd come across the like when some thug complained I didn't fight "fair". He didn't like it when I didn't use fisticuffs when he tried to bully me. Meanwhile, said thug had picked on me because I was smaller than him, and no match for him in brute strength.

"I will use what tools I have to counter a bully and feel no scruples about it." I said.

"Hmm." Damien said.

"What is this 'prize' they speak of, anyway?"

Damien sighed. "They assume Crystal is paying for your protection with her favors."

"The article writer raises an interesting point, Shifty," Tobias said from his perch.

"What's that?"

"A good luck charm could counter your jinxes." Tobias laughed.

"Which is why you must up your game and learn to cast death curses."

Damien snorted. "It'd never occur to that fool to research you and come prepared. He is a one-trick pony that only knows how to blast things while you've got three useful talents to your credit. Your intuition can sense the presence and strength of magic. You also have the author's voice trick and the ability to jinx people."

"Harry Hardwick will never be more than an enforcer for magicians smarter than him. He won't advance unless a mentor guides his career and that's a dangerous position to be in."

Which summed up my relationship with Damien. It was a temporary alliance. If I was lucky, he wouldn't be treacherous once my apprenticeship was done. We weren't friends, and he'd be looking out for his own interests once my term was over.

I sorted out the mail and saw I had another letter from Maximus.

I opened it. *Your presence at the Hellfire Club is requested. Young Hardwick is interested in a rematch, and so are other members of the Trade. Perhaps it's best to put everyone's doubts to rest?*

"What's that?" Damien asked.

"Maximus Worthington's sending me personalized junk mail now. He wants me to come back to the club and have a rematch with Harry."

Tobias clucked with satisfaction at this. "Showing mercy was a mistake. They won't stop harassing you until one of you is dead."

"So I've got to kill Harry Hardwick to end this? Maximus wants me to do this rematch in front of an audience."

Damien scowled. "An audience? He wishes you to perform like a parlor magician?"

"As far as I'm concerned, Maximus Worthington wishes to treat me even worse than a parlor magician." I said.

Damien frowned at this. "In what way?"

"A parlor magician would get a fee for his performance, Damien. Maximus is using me to get free publicity for his club. Yet offers me no compensation whatsoever."

Damien nodded "yes" at this. He took the letter from my hand and ripped it.

"You are to draft a response to the rematch challenge, but are to send it to Warlock Weekly's letters to the editor. This man wishes to goad you into giving free performances to his club of wannabes. We'll respond by shaming him in public."

"Your time is my time. I won't have it wasted on fruitless spectacles." Damien said.

Which is why I spent the afternoon crafting my letter to the editor in my office.

The Hellfire Club invited me to a rematch with Harry Hardwick, and I'm refusing it.

My apprenticeship doesn't obligate me to give free spectacles for a flesh peddler. Maximus Worthington doesn't have the courtesy to compensate for my work while he uses me to generate publicity for his club.

I know of a man who organizes blood sports at his club. This man makes sure his performers are willing to do their work and pays them for it. He also has a house doctor on hand to care for his fighters in case they get injured. I have more respect for this man than I do for Maximus Worthington.

Once I was satisfied with my letter, I sent it off. Maximus wanted to goad me in private, but I was exposing his ploys to the public.

MY RESPONSE WAS THE headline for Warlock's Weekly. Damien read it out to me. "Shelton Sharpe has overreached himself. He's trying to fight a master and not fellow apprentices. He sent an incendiary response to the Letters to the Editor page."

"Incendiary? That's exaggerating." I said.

I looked at the Letters to the Editor page and saw they printed my letter without editing it.

Damien sighed. "Most of the Trade sees the pursuit of money as a sign of dark side greed."

"So proper apprentices are supposed to be unpaid interns?" I snorted. "That's nothing but a scam to make sure only the already wealthy can afford to work their way through the Trade."

Damien nodded. "Or to foster dependence in talented novices, so they need a patron to cover their living expenses."

I HAD TO CATCH UP ON the yardwork after the exhibition. The cleaning wand meant I only had to spend one day dedicated to this chore to catch up. It would've taken at least two days of physical labor otherwise. I supervised the rake as it gathered fallen leaves.

The spell was more complicated than usual. I attached an illusion of a gardener raking the leaves. I was supposedly relaxing in a lawn chair under the gazebo. Though I appeared to be more focused on my gardener's work than a true man of leisure would be.

Scrappy in the meantime was relaxing in the shade. He liked to watch me work, even if he didn't want to work himself. Though he contributed by being a good mouser, scout and fetch for me when I needed it.

Scrappy let out a snarl. His fur was raised straight along his spine. I followed his gaze and saw there was a man at our gate on the street staring at the gardener. I recognized him from the image I'd seen from Crystal's letters. It was Maximus Worthington.

When he saw he had my attention, he snorted. He held up a walking cane, that looked too slim and decorative to be of use to anyone who needed it. I sought to make him move on with a pretext. "It's rude to criticize another man's servant." I spoke up.

"But it's below a premiere magician's dignity to use a cheap parlor trick."

Maximus grinned and pointed his wand toward my supposed gardener. The crystal at the top of wand glowed red. I held up the cleaning wand. It was useless against him, but he didn't know it.

He smirked. My hand wavered when my bluff was called. However, I wasn't alone. The cast-iron Mastiff doorknocker at the front door opened its eyes and glared at Maximus. This was more intimidating to him than my small talk rebuff.

The glow in the wand's crystal and the Mastiff's eyes increased in intensity as they stared at each other. My heart sped up. The Mastiff was capable, but I didn't want to risk causing a public spectacle.

I flicked the wand to my gardener projection and made it walk up to the gate and advance towards Maximus. Maximus was so engaged in the contest with the Mastiff he didn't notice what I was doing.

A flick of my wrist caused the gardener to use his rake's handle. I'd had to use the wand to energize a pounder to beat dust out of hanging rugs before. I'd built up the strength of these strikes.

It was just as well all the housework had given me practice. The gardener projection had enough force to knock the wand from Maximus's hand. The wand fell down, but its light shone through my gardener projection and caused it to disappear.

However, the wand's crystal shattered when it fell to the ground. The crystal shattered into fine sparks that died down to inert glass pieces.

Maximus shook his head and snorted. He looked up at me. I held the wand I had aloft. He frowned.

My heart pounded. I'd be in trouble if he didn't think I had a weapon grade wand. He took one long look at the wand then sighed before he walked away from the front gates.

The Mastiff gave a snort. Its nostrils flared as if it wanted to snort fire. "So you're good at something besides housework, Shifty."

Chapter 11-Now That You've Proven Yourself

The next morning I had more mail than usual to sort. There was a thick envelope from the Hellfire Club. I wondered if Maximus was resorting to lawfare since his attack hadn't worked.

"This can't be right. I don't know where Warlock's Weekly gets their information." Damien read over the latest headline in Warlock's Weekly for me. I'd laid it out for him, but hadn't read it myself yet.

"It says they have terminated Maximus Worthington from the Hellfire Club's management position. They ousted him with a 'lack of confidence' vote."

This news was wonderful for Crystal, but I found it hard to believe myself. "What does 'loss of confidence' mean?"

"It says his poor performance in a duel on my property made them reevaluate his fitness to lead the club." He read it out again.

"Oh," I shrugged.

Damien glanced up at me and his eyes narrowed, "What do you mean 'oh'"?

"He was here yesterday with his wand, as I did the yardwork." I began.

"He was here?" Damien repeated.

"He came when I was doing the yardwork with the cleaning wand. He left when I broke his wand," I said.

"Humph," Damien said. "Mastiff," he spoke aloud to our ward. "Is what he said true?"

"Yes." The voice boomed out.

"Hm," Damien grunted. "How did you do it?"

"Maximus came here with a wand while I was doing yardwork. The Mastiff stopped his attack. He concentrated on the Mastiff. I used a gardener projection to beat the wand out of his hand and knock it to the ground. That's when it broke."

Damien laughed. "I don't know if that means you're better than I think you are or Maximus is more careless than I thought he was."

I shrugged off this comment. "I never said I was some grand master."

Damien's brows rose. "He must've thought he could best you in a weak moment. However, it's not as if they will hold every battle under the rules of fair play."

"If he's gone, I wonder why the Hellfire Club sent me this envelope." I opened it to see that it contained Crystal's employment contract for the club with the word "VOID" stamped on it.

There was also a letter from Orion:

Mr. Sharpe

The Hellfire Club is under new management now. We're reevaluating Maximus Worthington's executive decisions, considering his poor performance record.

I have enclosed Crystal Moore's employment contract with the Hellfire Club. We have released her to your custody as the spoils of war.

I snorted. "Spoils of war? Crystal won't like that..."

That's why I only gave Crystal the voided contract and left out "the spoils of war" comment when I gave my last report. Her gratitude was so great she wrote me a generous cheque.

"I'll send Braun the brownie to help you with your housekeeping and yardwork. You're time's too important to waste on menial chores." she said.

"A brownie?" I wondered if it was a euphemism for some ethnic person or a person of color.

"Braun's not squeamish about working around dark magics. He prefers to work at night but will follow your orders as long as he respects you."

I accepted the card for the sake of politeness and took it home after I cashed in the cheque at the bank.

THAT AFTERNOON I TOOK the precaution of informing the Mastiff of our planned visitor. "There's a brownie coming to fill the housekeeper vacancy. Let them in and send him to my office."

The Mastiff gave a barking laugh at this. "A brownie? A brownie?"

"Will you do it or not?" I snapped.

The Mastiff gave one last guffaw. "Yes, I've got to see this."

They had warned me Braun preferred the night shift, but it miffed me when he didn't come until dusk came. I had to set my fire in the room and was disgusted when I saw the ball of hair on the hearthrug.

"DID YOU COUGH UP ANOTHER hairball, Scrappy?" I asked my lazy familiar, pointing to the offensive hairball.

He looked up at me and the hairball and hissed.

I jumped when the hairball moved.

"You asked for me?" The tone was deeper than I expected. It issued out from the 'hairball'.

"You're Braun?" I asked.

"Yes," he nodded.

"Crystal recommended you to me."

He nodded, "As pretty and fine as crystal ware. I wasn't able to protect her in the daytime."

It took self-control not to laugh at him. "You were her protector?"

"Not the kind that pays her bills or sponsors her in Society. The best I could do was ward her against magical threats."

"All the wards I know demand payment for their services. What are your terms?" I wondered if I'd be stuck with another trick that demanded blood from me.

"I took a bowl of cream, a platter of oatcakes and a smile from Crystal. We fae creatures are drawn to beauty, even if we're not pretty ourselves. "

I smiled. "I doubt you'd take similar terms from me."

He huffed. "I want the bowl of cream and platter of oatcakes at any rate. Plus, I insist on a night shift. I won't work any daytime hours for you like I did for her."

"Agreed. That'll lighten my workload, at least." I said.

"It'll free up time for your studies. Everyone in the Trade is itching to see how far you'll go when you can knuckle down."

It was more likely Damien would expect me to do more freelancing if I spent less time on housework.

INDEED, DAMIEN RECEIVED another letter from Mathilde. "Mathilde wants to know if there are other hostessing contracts available to buy out."

I was drinking coffee and shrugged. "I can only protect one woman at a time. I didn't ask."

"You're my man of business, and it's only natural for you to make an inquiry for me." Damien said.

"Then this is business. I don't have to fight duels for this?"

Damien snorted. "Refer them to me if they want to put up the contracts as competition trophies."

I followed Damien's advice, and I presented the list of contracts Mathilde wanted. Orion said, "You ask for too much."

"I'm acting as Damien Rathschild's man of business in this venture. He sent me to negotiate a suitable price for him, but he said he'd be willing to accept any challenges you want to issue."

"Then he's the one who'll have to face me." Harry snorted from the couch.

THEY OUTRAGED DAMIEN with the counteroffer. We had to go to the club, and he insisted I wear my best evening clothes. "I want you to look presentable when you deliver the contracts to Mathilde tonight."

The club was even dingier under his withering glance. His tailoring made their foppish clothes look shabby. He transfixed Stella. Her eyes were wide and dark with fear and excitement.

He refused to carry a wand. "I won't need it." He said with a sneer.

Harry clutched his wand so hard his knuckles turned white.

"You may go first," Orion said as he gestured at the dummies.

A pillar of fire erupted from the ground and engulfed Damien's dummy. It incinerated it to black ash in an instant.

Harry's mouth gaped open at this.

"Give Shelton all the contracts on the list."

Orion followed Damien's instructions, and I made sure to double-check the contracts and put them in order.

Stella proffered lemonade to Damien as he waited for Orion and I to finish our business. "Humph." But Damien still took the drink. He wasn't as overexerted as Harry would've been but needed to cool down.

After I counted and checked off every contract on the list I said, "I've collected them all."

"Then we can leave now."

Harry went up to Damien. "We're looking for a new executive officer for the Hellfire Club-"

Damien cut him off with a disdainful glance at the people and surroundings of the club. He gestured to me. "I prefer quality to quantity."

Harry bit his lip and held back the retort he wanted to make.

MATHILDE MADE US GUESTS of honor at her latest cotillion.

"The Watchers need not be concerned about the Hellfire Club. They're a sad little group now, and not a coven." Damien said.

"The Hellfire Club members would be better off getting individual attention from masters. Not competing for the attention of one master."

Damien shrugged. "Let the Watchers make overtures at the more promising members if they want. I'm not into giving away charity."

Fletcher said, "What about paying it forward."

Damien sniffed. "I believe in paybacks for good or ill. Not 'paying it forward'".

He walked off when a Diamond asked him for a dance. Most men had to ask them. Unless the Diamond wanted to distract the man, or she was eager for his company. In Damien's case, it was a little of both. Fletcher shook his head at this.

Mathilde spoke to me once Damien was distracted. "In your case, I'd search out further education opportunities. I'm head of the Enchantress Guild. I give advanced classes for the top students, but each Diamond gets her own mentor."

"Not even you could teach me how to enchant anyone." I shrugged.

"There are masters among the Watchers interested in refining all your skillsets. That author's voice trick is enough to make you an expert witness. The Watchers want you to be certified as a notary republic or handwriting expert, so they can call on you as one.

They'd be willing to buy you the best scrying mirror possible to use against anonymous notes."

I nodded. "That seems harmless enough. You must discuss my training program with Damien. I'm willing to network during my apprenticeship, but not to trade up."

Mathilde smile was so dazzling I glimpsed the glamour she must've had in her youth. "Then that makes Damien Rathschild the most spoiled master in the Trade."

About the Author

Cathy Smith is a Mohawk writer who lives on a Status Reservation on the Canadian Side of the Border.

She is proud of her people's heritage, and has an interest in the traditions of other cultures. Most of her works to date have been based on the folkloric traditions she's studied. Science fiction and fantasy strikes her as the folklore of the modern age, and she considers both genres a natural choice for her own writings.

You can follow her at:

Wordpress: bit.ly/2e41qWT

Facebook: bit.ly/2dP3rXd

Twitter: @khiatons

Instagram:@cathy2891

Tumblr: bit.ly/2G3dEjo

Tiktok: bit.ly/3KoGwBf

Sign up to the Cathy Smith-Khiatons-I Write Substack https://bit.ly/4qATMGH to receive news and excerpts of new publications and promotions.